Magic
Animal Friends

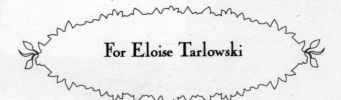

For Eloise Tarlowski

Special thanks to Valerie Wilding

ORCHARD BOOKS

First published in Great Britain in 2017 by The Watts Publishing Group

1 3 5 7 9 10 8 6 4 2

Text copyright © Working Partners Ltd 2017
Illustrations copyright © Orchard Books 2017

The moral rights of the author and illustrator have been asserted.
All characters and events in this publication, other than those clearly in the public domain,
are fictitious and any resemblance to real persons, living or dead, is purely coincidental.

All rights reserved.
No part of this publication may be reproduced, stored in a retrieval system, or transmitted, in any form
or by any means, without the prior permission in writing of the publisher, nor be otherwise circulated in
any form of binding or cover other than that in which it is published and without a similar condition
including this condition being imposed on the subsequent purchaser.

A CIP catalogue record for this book is available from the British Library.

ISBN 978 1 40834 607 5

Printed in Great Britain

MIX
Paper from
responsible sources
FSC® C104740
FSC
www.fsc.org

The paper and board used in this book are made from wood from responsible sources.

Orchard Books
An imprint of Hachette Children's Group
Part of The Watts Publishing Group Limited
Carmelite House, 50 Victoria Embankment, London EC4Y 0DZ

An Hachette UK Company
www.hachette.co.uk
www.hachettechildrens.co.uk

Anna Fluffyfoot Goes for Gold

Daisy Meadows

ORCHARD

Sunshine
Meadow

Honey
Tree

Goldie's Grotto

Toadstool
Cafe

Toadstool Glade

Mrs Taptree's
Library

Friendship
Tree

Parasol
Tree

Library

Grizelda's
Workshop

Butterfly
Bowery

Rushing Rapids

Spar
Fall

Heart Trees

Nibblesqueak Bakery

Map of Friendship Forest

Can you keep a secret? I thought you could!

Then I'll tell you about an enchanted wood.

It lies through the door in the old oak tree,

Let's go there now - just follow me!

We'll find adventure that never ends,

And meet the Magic Animal Friends!

Love,
Goldie the Cat

Story One
Petal Path

CHAPTER ONE

Sunshine Meadow

"The stable looks fantastic!" Lily Hart
said to her best friend, Jess Forester.

Lily's parents ran the Helping Paw
Wildlife Hospital in a barn in their
garden, and the girls adored working
with the poorly animals. Today they
were helping Mr and Mrs Hart in a field

behind the garden where there was a paddock with a stable. They'd just finished putting down a bed of wood shavings.

"It's great!" said Jess. "Starshine Sparkle's going to love it!"

Starshine Sparkle was a retired racehorse who belonged to a man in the local village. Now she wasn't racing any more, the stable would be her new home.

Mrs Hart smiled and pointed to the

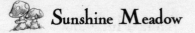

garden over the fence. "We've got an audience!"

The animals in the hospital's outdoor pens were watching curiously. Three baby rabbits peeped out from their hutch. In the next pen, a tiny squirrel sat in her feed bowl to watch. A white goat kid and a caramel-coloured calf stood beneath a shady tree, keeping an eye on the activity.

Lily laughed. "Starshine Sparkle will have lots of company here!"

Mr Hart brought over a water bucket. "Starshine Sparkle's owner, Tom, says he'll visit her whenever he can," he said. "She's

got a lovely paddock to gallop around, so she'll be perfectly happy."

Mrs Hart closed the stable door. "We'll sweep up," she said, looking at the hay wisps blowing about. "You girls have worked so hard. Off you go — enjoy this lovely summer day!"

"Thanks, Mum!" said Lily.

"See you!" said Jess.

"Racehorses must have exciting lives," said Lily, as they walked across the garden towards the house. "If only Starshine Sparkle could talk, like the animals in Friendship Forest!"

Friendship Forest was the girls' secret. It was a magical place where all the animals lived in little cottages or dens, and drank blackberry tea in the Toadstool Café. Best of all, they could talk! Jess and Lily had made many friends in the forest, and had lots of exciting adventures.

The girls grinned at each other as they thought of it. Then suddenly there was a flash of gold at the other side of the garden.

"Look!" Jess cried, pointing across the lawn to Mrs Hart's strawberry bed.

A beautiful cat slipped between the

 13

plump, leafy plants and ran towards the girls. She had soft golden fur and eyes as green as freshly mown grass.

"Goldie!" Lily cried.

The cat pressed against their legs, purring.

The girls stroked her, glancing at each other in excitement. Goldie was their magical friend!

"She's come to take us back to Friendship Forest!" said Jess.

Goldie darted to Brightley Stream at the bottom of the garden. She leapt over the stepping stones that crossed the water,

and into Brightley Meadow.

The girls ran after her as she raced towards a lifeless old tree.

As soon as Goldie reached it, the tree burst into life. Every branch sprouted bright green leaves, and bees buzzed among pale pink blooms. Butterflies danced over scarlet poppies growing in the grass below, and two chaffinches chirped merrily as they swooped around the tree.

As Jess and Lily caught up with Goldie, she put a paw to the trunk. Words appeared in the bark, and the girls read them aloud together.

"Friend … ship For … est!"

Instantly, a door appeared in the tree.

Shivering with excitement, Jess reached for the leaf-shaped handle and opened it. Golden light spilled out.

The girls followed the cat into the soft warm glow. Straight away, they felt the tingle that told them they were shrinking, just a little.

When the light faded, they found themselves in a sunlit forest glade. Nearby, Goldie stood upright, almost as tall as the girls, and she wore her glittery scarf.

"Welcome back to Friendship Forest,"
she said in her soft voice.

The girls hugged her. "It's lovely to see
you again!" said Jess.

"Is Grizelda causing more trouble?"
Lily asked.

Grizelda was a horrible witch who

wanted to take Friendship Forest over
from the animals, so she could have it to
herself. So far the girls had managed to
stop her evil plans, but Grizelda never
gave up.

"We've not seen Grizelda for ages," said
Goldie, "thank goodness! No, I've brought
you here to take you to the Friendship
Forest Sports Day!"

Lily's eyes sparkled. "That sounds
fantastic!"

Jess grinned. "I bet it's not an ordinary
sports day like we have at our school!"

"Probably not," said Goldie with a

 18

smile. "The Friendship Forest Sports Day is magical! The races aren't like any ordinary races. Come on, I'll tell you all about it when we get there."

The forest was unusually quiet. As the friends passed the animals' cottages, there were no cheery greetings from the doors. The Toadstool Café, which was usually buzzing, had no lights on at all, the shutters were over the windows and a 'closed' sign hung outside. It was as if the whole Forest was empty.

"Where is everyone?" Lily wondered. "Are they at the Sports Day already?"

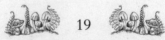

Goldie nodded. "Yes," she said. She pushed between some jellyberry bushes, their fat fruit almost bursting open as they brushed past. "Look!"

Sunshine Meadow was usually ablaze with bright yellow, orange and red flowers. But the grass had been mown for the events and the meadow was filled with animals.

Refreshment stalls stood around

the edge, selling delicious food, like
warm hazelnut and banana pancakes,
and coconut cream tarts topped with
blueberries. Little tables and chairs stood
nearby, with striped parasols to shade
them from the sun. Animals milled about,
munching snacks or sipping orange and
lemon smoothies.

In the middle of the meadow, a short
racetrack was marked out with orange

flower petals. To one side was a fence, a tunnel and other obstacles. On the other side was a tall stone tower.

Jess noticed a list of races pinned on an easel. "Petal Path," she read. "Tumble Run. Tricky Tower." She grinned at Lily. "It's like Goldie said, these aren't ordinary races at all."

"You're right. It's nothing like the sports day at school!" agreed Lily.

The girls could see lots of their friends stretching and warming up.

Bella Tabbypaw the kitten, wearing sparkly pink leg warmers, waved. "Hello,

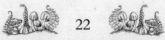

Jess and Lily!"

Other animals waved, too. The
Twinkletail mice were wearing tiny
matching yellow T-shirts and shorts, with
holes in the backs so their tails could
pop out. Chloe Slipperslide the otter was
dressed in a sleek sea-green leotard.

A few metres away a tortoiseshell kitten
was doing star jumps. Then she did five
perfect back flips
towards them, but
on the last one she
flipped right into
Lily's leg! The girls

giggled as the kitten collapsed into a ball of fluff.

"Sorry, sorry, sorry!" the kitten said. She sat up and gasped. "You're Jess and Lily! I've heard all about you! I'm Anna Fluffyfoot. Hello, Goldie! "

The kitten's dappled fur gleamed in the sunlight. Her sparkly jumpsuit was the exact colour of Goldie's green eyes, and she wore matching wristbands.

"It's great to meet you, Anna," said Jess. "I love your outfit."

"Are you excited about Sports Day?" Lily asked the kitten.

Anna nodded,
shook her head, then
nodded again, as if she wasn't sure.
"Sort of," she said, twanging a wristband.
"I'm a bit nervous. But I've been
practising hard. There's a brilliant prize
for the winning team. Come and see!"

Anna led Jess, Lily and Goldie to a
tree at the far end of the meadow. It
was covered with delicate golden leaves,
and on one of the branches was a single
beautiful pink blossom.

"This is the Wishing Tree," said Anna.

 25

"And this" – she pointed to the pink blossom – "is the Wishing Blossom. It's the big prize. There are three races, so whoever wins most of them will be declared Sports Day champions and will get the blossom. It grants the winning team one wish."

"Wow!" said Jess. "You mean they can wish for anything?"

Anna nodded. "Anything! And it will come true."

The girls were amazed. What a wonderful prize for winning Sports Day – your own special wish!

CHAPTER TWO

Grizelda's Wish

"What a fantastic prize!" said Lily.

"A bit different from the stickers we get at school," said Jess with a smile.

"We also have medals for the winner of each race," said Anna. "But the overall winners get the Wishing Blossom. I think my team has a good chance of winning.

Come and meet them!"

Goldie and the girls followed Anna
across the meadow.

"There they are, practising their jumps!"
she said, pointing. "We're Team Flower
Power."

Jess and Lily were thrilled to see that
Anna's teammates were old friends of
theirs.

"It's Evie Scruffypup and Hannah
Honeypaw!" cried Jess, waving to a
black-and-white puppy and a cuddly
brown bear, both wearing flowery
running shorts.

 28

"And Sophie Flufftail," said Lily, waving
to a squirrel in a pink-and-white striped
headband.

The girls hugged all their friends, but
they noticed that Anna looked rather
worried. They took her aside.

"What's wrong?" Lily asked.

"I'm nervous," said Anna. "Evie,
Hannah and Sophie all did really well
last year, but I was too little to take part.

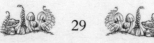

They're so good at sports – I'm worried
I'll let my team down."

Jess hugged the kitten. "It doesn't matter

whether you win
or lose," she said.
"Having fun together
is much more
important."

Anna nodded but
didn't look too sure.

Lily comforted her. "You'll—"

But she was interrupted by frightened
shouts coming from the middle of the
meadow. The three friends looked around

and saw the animals huddled together, a yellow-green orb of light hovering above them.

"Oh no!" cried Jess. "It's Grizelda!"

"Keep back!" Lily cried, pulling Anna behind her.

The orb burst in a shower of smelly sparks and there stood Grizelda. Locks of green hair swished around her bony face. She wore a purple tunic over skinny black trousers, and high-heeled boots with sharply pointed toes.

The younger animals squealed and squeaked in alarm, huddling behind their

31

frightened parents.

"Ha ha!" shrieked the witch. "You animals and your silly Sports Day! I'll show you! My team will win all the races. Then you'll have to give me the Wishing Blossom and I'll wish to have Friendship Forest all to myself!"

"Not while we're here!" cried Lily, shielding Anna from the witch.

Hannah, Evie and Sophie bunched together, bravely facing Grizelda.

"We won't let you win!" Evie Scruffypup shouted. "You won't beat Team Flower Power!"

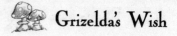

"I won't need to beat you, silly puppy!"
Grizelda cackled. She punched a fist into
the air and chanted:

"Flower Power, you might have heart,

But there's no winner here.

I'll make sure you don't take part.

Flower Power — disappear!"

She lowered her fist and pointed a bony finger at the three terrified animals.

In a puff of dirty grey smoke, Evie, Hannah and Sophie vanished.

CHAPTER THREE

Wolf Cubs!

"Grizelda! What have you done?" Lily
shouted angrily.

The witch screamed with laughter.

Jess clutched Anna's paw. The kitten was
trembling, but she yelled, "Bring back my
teammates!"

Grizelda turned her scornful gaze on

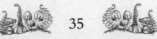

Anna. "That's not happening, kitty!" she snarled. "But I'll show you my teammates. Here come Team Snappyteeth!"

Four grey wolf cubs burst from the surrounding trees. They hurtled towards Grizelda, howling at everyone they passed. The littlest animals started to whimper and cry.

Grizelda smiled meanly. "Say hello to Dash, Flash, Crash and Smash!"

A cub with a black patch over one eye, and another with one white ear, wagged their tails and barked.

"These two are Dash and Flash. They're so fast they'll outrun any of you animals," Grizelda sneered. "Crash!"

A cub with a stubby tail howled.

"Crash is nimble and quick and can cope with any obstacle," said Grizelda. "He has excellent balance. Smash!"

A cub with one brown eye and one green eye howled.

"Smash could climb the tallest tree in the forest faster than anyone," said

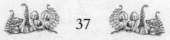

the witch. "None of you can beat Team

Snappyteeth!"

Jess clenched her fists. "If

you're hoping to ruin Sports

Day, Grizelda, you

can't. We won't let

you!"

"I can do

what I like!" the

witch snapped. "Team Snappyteeth will

win the Wishing Blossom for me. Then I'll

wish away all you horrid animals!"

She snapped her fingers and vanished

in a burst of stinking yellow sparks.

Team Snappyteeth ran over to an abandoned picnic basket. They tucked in, barging each other out of the way to get to the cakes and sandwiches.

"Come with us!" Lily called to the dazed animals. She and Jess led them away from Team Snappyteeth to the edge of the meadow.

"Whatever happens," Lily told them, "Grizelda and those bad wolf cubs mustn't win. If she gets the Wishing Blossom, you'll all be magicked away from your homes. For ever."

"How can we stop them winning?"

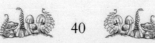

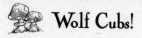

asked Mr Paddlefoot the beaver.

"Will Sports Day have to be cancelled?" asked Lily.

Mr Cleverfeather the elderly owl waddled forward, his wingtips tucked into his waistcoat pockets. "Lo, Nilly," he said, muddling his words as usual. "I mean, no Lily, we can't cancel it. The Wishing Blossom is enchanted. It must be won. If we don't compete, all the wolf cubs will need to do is finish the races. Then the Blishing Wossom will be theirs."

"In that case," said Jess, "the only way to stop Team Snappyteeth is to

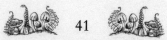

beat them." She glared as the wolf cubs sauntered past, eating stolen cream buns.

The animals whispered amongst themselves, looking worried. Then Mr Muddlepup said, "Those wolf cubs are so badly behaved, and our teams saw how fast they can run. Nobody wants to compete against Team Snappyteeth. They're too scared."

Goldie and the girls were dismayed. It looked as if Grizelda would win.

Lily glanced at Jess. "We have to find the rest of Team Flower Power."

Mr Cleverfeather shook his head

sorrowfully. "There's toe nime. I mean
no time. The first race starts in a few
minutes."

"If no one else will compete," said Jess,
"Lily, Goldie and I will join Team Flower
Power."

"We still need
a fourth team
member," Lily said,
looking around.

Anna slipped a
quivering paw into
Lily's hand. "You've
got me," she said in

a shaky voice. "I'll take part, too. I won't let my teammates down."

"Great!" said Jess and the watching animals cheered and clapped.

Anna glanced at the Wishing Tree. "When the Wishing Blossom lights up, it'll be time for the Petal Path race."

"Jess can run that," said Lily. "She's a fast sprinter."

Anna shook her head. "The Petal Path is a six-legged race," she explained. "Goldie and I can each tie one of our front paws together, and one of our back paws, and run like that."

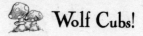

"Like a three-legged race!" said Jess.

"Let's have a quick practice, Anna," said Goldie.

Mr Cleverfeather produced some ribbons from his waistcoat pocket. "My latest invention," he said. "Running Ribbons! Lake a took. I mean, take a look."

He touched a silvery ribbon to Anna's front paw. It sprang to life, winding itself around her leg and Goldie's, too.

Once their back legs were also bound together, they set off and immediately fell over.

The wolf cubs, who were lolling on the grass, burst out laughing.

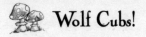 **Wolf Cubs!**

"We must get the hang of this before the Wishing Blossom lights up," said Goldie. "That's when the race will start."

They tried again and were tottering along when Dash and Flash raced across the grass.

"Watch out!" cried Jess.

The wolf cubs snapped and pulled at the Running Ribbons.

"We'll stop you starting," Dash laughed.

"Losers!" Flash sniggered.

Goldie pulled Anna away from the cubs, but she lost her balance because one leg was tied to the kitten's.

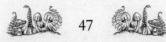

Over she went.

As Jess and Lily ran to help, Goldie gave

a sharp cry.

"Ow! Ow! Me-ow!"

CHAPTER FOUR

Teamwork

Goldie was clearly badly hurt, holding her leg and wincing in pain. Jess and Lily untied the Running Ribbons and were trying to comfort her, when a little grey owl skittered over. She carried a basket with a red cross stencilled on it.

"Matilda Fluffywing!" said Jess. "Thank

 49

goodness you're here!"

"Can you help Goldie?" asked Lily.

Matilda's parents were doctors, and they'd taught her all about first aid. She examined Goldie's paw, then sighed heavily. "I'm afraid you've sprained it," she said. "No racing for you today."

Goldie's green eyes brimmed with tears. "Oh no!" she said. "How will we win the Petal Path race now?"

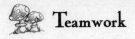

Anna looked horrified. "If we don't race, the wolf cubs will win!" Her eyes filled with tears, too.

"Don't cry!" said Jess. "I've got an idea. Mr Cleverfeather," she called, "could Lily and I run the Petal Path as a three-legged race?"

"There's nothing in the rules to say you can't," he said. "So yes, moo yay. I mean, you may."

He threw a golden Running Ribbon to the girls. It wrapped magically around one of each of their ankles, binding them securely together.

"Hurry," he said. "The Blishing Wossom's beginning to glow!"

The girls scuttled to the starting line. Dash and Flash were already lined up, each with a front paw and a back paw tied together with string. They growled at Lily and Jess, but the girls just ignored them.

Jess looked at the orange flower petals marking out the track. They didn't go very far. "It's a short race," she said.

Anna nervously twanged her wristband. "It's a magical race," she said. "Once you start, the petals will move to show you the

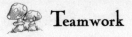

next bit of the course."

Lily and Jess glanced at the wolf cubs, who crouched down, ready to run. Would they be as fast, Lily wondered, with their legs tied together? She knew she and Jess would be quite slow.

Dash pawed the start line. "You'll never win," he growled.

"Silly girls," added Flash.

Lily and Jess felt very nervous as they watched the Wishing Tree.

Suddenly, the blossom lit up so brightly it cast a pink glow across Sunshine Meadow.

"It's time for the Petal Path race!" said Mr Cleverfeather, raising the starting flag. "On more yarks! I mean, on your marks! Steady … ready …"

He swung the flag down. "Go!"

The girls put their arms around each

 54

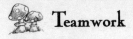

other's waists and ran. They were slow,
stumbling as they tried to keep in time
with each other. As they neared the end
of the track, more flower petals appeared,
going off in a slightly different direction.
The track kept growing in front of them,
but it was twisty-turny, and they only
knew which way to go when the petals
showed them.

Lily glanced back and saw that the
wolves were close behind.

"They're going to catch us up," she
panted. "If only we could go faster!"

"I know how!" cried Anna. The kitten

was sprinting alongside the race track. "Count your steps – one two, one two, one two …"

Lily and Jess matched their pace to Anna's counts. Now their legs were all moving perfectly in time.

"We're speeding up!" cried Jess.

"Hooray!" cheered the watching crowd.

Lily looked back again. Dash and Flash were pushing and shoving each other as they ran.

"You're too slow!" grumbled Dash.

"No, you're too fast!" snapped Flash.

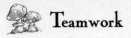

"Ow! You pushed me over!"

"Didn't! You dragged me down!"

The girls were pulling ahead.

"We're going to win!" said Lily.

But Jess felt her leg knock against something. "Ow!" she cried out. She stumbled, bringing Lily down, too. They hit the ground with a thump.

The crowd gasped in dismay.

When the girls sat up, they saw Smash grinning at them. She had a long stick in her mouth.

"You tripped me!" Jess said furiously.

"Cheat!" cried Lily.

The girls scrambled to help each other up. But Dash and Flash ran past them, sprinting off into the distance along the Petal Path.

Smash howled with laughter. "You'll never beat Team Snappyteeth!"

Lily clutched Jess's waist. "We must keep trying!" she cried. They set off again.

"Go, Flower Power!" Anna yelled. "You can do it!"

Jess gritted her teeth. "Anna's right," she said. "We've got to – for Friendship Forest!"

CHAPTER FIVE

Flower Power!

"One two, one two, one two ..." yelled
Anna, her counting getting faster and
faster as she sprinted along beside the
girls.

Jess and Lily were soon gaining on
Team Snappyteeth once more. The wolves
were fast runners, but they kept barging

into each other.

"They're not working as a team," Jess panted.

Dash looked around and saw the girls. "Faster!" he yelped. "They're catching up!"

But Flash swerved around to look too – yanking Dash with her. With a furious howl, Dash fell, his paws scrabbling at the air. He knocked Flash over and the two cubs collapsed in a jumble of legs, tails and yelps.

"Come on!" cried Lily. "Now's our chance, Jess!"

The girls shot past Dash and Flash. Ahead, a line of petals formed the finish line. They stormed towards it.

"One two, one two, one two," yelled Anna. "You've nearly done it!"

"Whooo! Go, Team Flower Power!" the crowd shouted.

Jess and Lily rushed across the finishing line. They jumped for joy, forgetting

their legs were tied together, and fell in a happy, tangled heap.

The watching animals shrieked with delight.

"Woo-woo-wooo!"

"Go, Flower! Go, Power!"

While the wolf cubs picked angrily at the knotted string around their legs, Anna did a dance of delight.

"Yay, Lily and Jess!" she cried. "You did it!"

"We did the running," said Lily, "but your counting kept us together."

The sound of angry howls reached

the friends. They glanced across at Team
Snappyteeth. Dash and Flash were still
tied up together, with Smash and Crash
scowling at them.

"You should have
run faster!" Smash
complained.

"Those girls have
only got two legs
each," Crash grumbled.
"You've got four!"

Just then, Goldie
hobbled over on
wooden crutches.

"Congratulations!" she said, as they hugged her.

"How is your paw?" asked Lily, as Goldie sat on the grass.

"Much better," she said, "thanks to Matilda's clever bandaging."

Jess started to undo the Running Ribbon. The moment she touched it, the ribbon untied itself and flew across the meadow to where Mr Cleverfeather sat in a folding chair.

Dash and Flash had untied themselves too. All four of the wolf cubs prowled towards the friends.

"You won't win the next race," said
Smash.

"We will," said Jess.

"Oh no, you won't," said Crash. "I'll
make sure of it!"

The four cubs slunk away into the trees.

"Huh! We'd better watch those wolves carefully," said Lily. "They're bound to cheat again."

"And we have to find Anna's missing teammates," Jess said. "Their parents must be so worried."

"You're right," said Goldie, hobbling along. "But there isn't time before the next race. We'll have to look for them when Sports Day is over."

Anna's face lit up. "I have a better idea. If we win the Wishing Blossom, then we can wish my teammates back!"

"That's an amazing idea, Anna!" Jess cried. "We'll be beating Grizelda twice, then – stopping her from getting the Wishing Blossom, and bringing back Team Flower Power."

"We just need to win one more race and the Wishing Blossom will be ours," said Lily.

Anna smiled. "Now you've joined Team Flower Power, we can do it!"

"We can," said Jess. "With teamwork!"

Story Two
Tumble Run

CHAPTER ONE

Worried Anna

Goldie sat at a little table to rest her
sprained paw while the others went to the
refreshment stalls for a quick snack. Jess,
Lily, Anna and Goldie were thrilled that
Team Flower Power had beaten Grizelda's
wolf cubs and won the first of the three
Friendship Forest Sports Day races.

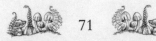

"Everything's so yummy," said Jess, stopping at the Prettywhiskers' Purrfect Ice Cream stall. "Hazelnut Crunch, Lemon and Lime Delight, Strawberry Cream Swirl ... Mmmm!"

"I'm glad you've joined Team Flower Power," said Anna. "If we beat Team Snappyteeth once more, we'll win the Wishing Blossom."

"And stop Grizelda getting her hands on it and wishing all the animals out of Friendship Forest," said Lily.

"Then we can wish for Anna's missing teammates to come back," said Jess.

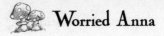

They visited the bakery stall, where Mrs Nibblesqueak the hamster was heaping cupcakes on to a plate.

"Could we have four raspberry meringue puffs, please?" Lily asked.

"Certainly," said Mrs Nibblesqueak, loading them on to a tray. "We all want you to win, so here's a great snack to keep you going!" She added a piled-up plate to the tray.

 73

"My Zippy Zappy Flapjacks! They're bursting with oats, nuts, honey and cherries!"

"Yum!" said Lily.

Mrs Nibblesqueak poured banana smoothie into four coconut shells and set them on the tray.

"Thanks!" said Jess. "We'll have lots of energy after this!"

They settled down in the sunshine with Goldie, who explained about the next race as they ate.

"The Tumble Run is an obstacle course," Goldie said. She pointed across

the meadow to a very narrow fence. "First you walk along that fence and try not to tumble off."

"That looks difficult," said Lily. "What's next?"

"The Jumping Tree," said Goldie, pointing at a huge tree with spreading branches. "You leap three times from branch to branch without tumbling down. Then you slither through that hollow tree trunk, like going through a tunnel ..."

She glanced at the girls' faces. "What's wrong?"

"Lily and I are too big for this race,"

 75

said Jess. "We might manage to walk along the fence, just – but if we grab those branches, we'll drag them down. And we'd never wriggle through that hollow tree trunk." She turned to Anna. "I'm so sorry."

Goldie looked disappointed. "And I can't do it with a sprained paw."

Anna's whiskers twitched with worry. "I wish Hannah, Evie and Sophie were here," she said.

"But you can do it!" said Goldie. "You're small and light – and you're a cat! You're perfect for the Tumble Run."

"Perfect? Me?" Anna started to shake

her head, then stopped. "Well ... maybe I can do it ... I might not be as fast as my usual teammates, but I've been practising." She smiled nervously. "If you cheer me on, I'll do my best to beat those wolf cubs!" Anna took a bite of her Zippy Zappy Flapjack

Just then two dogs came towards them. One was black and brown, and carried

a huge picnic basket. The other was
brown and white and wore a wide yellow
sunhat.

"Hello, Mr and Mrs Snuffynose," Goldie
said, and introduced the girls.

The dogs looked worried. Mr
Snuffynose said,
"You haven't seen
our four little
puppies, have you?
They were here in
Sunshine Meadow
when we arrived,
but now we can't

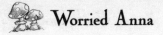

find them anywhere."

"They were really looking forward to a lovely picnic," said Mrs Snuffynose, her brow wrinkled with worry. "I can't imagine where they've run off to."

"We'll look out for them," Jess promised.

"Thank you," said Mr Snuffynose. "It shouldn't be too hard to find four noisy, playful puppies."

The dogs left, paw-in-paw, with drooping ears.

"Poor Mr and Mrs Snuffynose," said Anna. She looked up at the girls with wide eyes. "What if Grizelda's magicked the puppies away, like she did to Hannah, Evie and Sophie?"

"Don't worry," Lily told her. "The puppies are probably off playing with the other baby animals. If they don't turn up, we'll find them after the races."

Anna nodded, but her eyes were still big with worry. "What if I mess up the Tumble Run?" she said. "I know I won't be fast enough. Or nimble enough. I'm just not good enough."

Jess glanced at Lily. Anna had seemed quite confident about the race a few

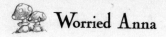

minutes before. Why was she acting differently?

Lily hugged the trembling kitten. "Anna, you were just telling us that you thought you could do the race," she said. "Why are you so nervous all of a sudden?"

Anna's eyes filled with tears. "I don't know," she said.

Jess gave her a hug. "You'll be fine. We'll be cheering you on, remember?"

Anna shook her head. "I'm scared I'll tumble off the fence and Team Snappyteeth will win the Wishing

Blossom and Grizelda will wish everyone out of Friendship Forest and ... oh ..."

She put her paws over her face and sobbed. "I know it'll let everyone down. But I can't do the race!"

CHAPTER TWO

Very Scary Cherry

Lily passed Anna her flapjack. "You've only eaten half," she said. "Perhaps with a bit more energy, you'll—"

"Wait a moment!" said Jess. She showed Lily and Goldie her flapjack, which was dotted with plump red cherries. "Now look at Anna's."

 83

The others peered at the flapjack in
Anna's shaky paw. The pieces of cherry
sticking out of Anna's flapjack were dark
purple, with green flecks.

"Her cherries are different," said Lily.

"Hmm. Something's not right," said
Goldie. "Let's ask Mrs Nibblesqueak
about them."

Jess held the kitten's shaky paw as she and Lily hurried to the bakery stall. Goldie followed on her crutches, and the four wolf cubs slunk behind her.

When Mrs Nibblesqueak saw the remains of Anna's flapjack, she was horrified.

"We'd never use those cherries in our flapjacks," she said, picking out a piece. "I've seen them before in Cherry Tree Corner. This," she said, "is a Very Scary Cherry!"

Goldie had caught up. "What does it do?" she asked.

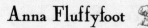

"Whoever eats it becomes frightened," replied Mrs Nibblesqueak.

Jess scooped Anna into her arms. "No wonder you're nervous!" she said, as the kitten clung to her.

The friends heard howls of laughter and turned to see Dash, Smash, Flash and Crash rolling on the floor. They all had strange purple marks on their front paws.

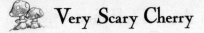

"Hee hee!" chuckled Dash. "Not so brave now, are you, little kitty?"

Lily was furious. "You stuck those bits of bad cherry on Anna's snack bar while we were talking! I know you did! You've got cherry juice stains on your paws!"

Smash was laughing so much it took her a moment to catch her breath. Then she said, "Now the kitten is a – ha ha ha – a scaredy cat!"

Anna was in tears again. "See, I'm not brave and I am scared." She buried her little face beneath Jess's chin. "I can't do the Tumble Run."

Crash laughed. "That's good news!" he said. "It means I'll win. In fact, Team Snappyteeth can't lose!"

The girls and Goldie left the howling wolves, and went to the edge of the meadow to talk. Jess carried poor trembling Anna.

"We've got to stop the cherry's magic," said Lily. "And we've got to do it before that blossom starts to glow!"

CHAPTER THREE

Olivia's Brainwave

"OK, who's got any ideas?" asked Jess.

"Hmm ..." Lily said. "As the Very Scary Cherry came from Cherry Tree Corner, maybe we'll find something there to make Anna brave again."

"It's worth a try," said Goldie. "Come on – it's not far."

 89

With Goldie hobbling as fast as possible on her crutches, they set off.

Cherry Tree Corner was in a sunny clearing, surrounded by tall fir trees. The cherry trees were in seven neat rows. Some were smothered in scented pink blossoms, while bunches of ripe, juicy cherries hung from others. The girls had been here before. They knew there were cherries that turned animals' fur pink for a while, ones that turned noses bright green, and another type that had once given Jess pointy ears!

A small animal was filling a basket

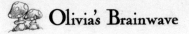

with bright red cherries.

"It's Olivia Nibblesqueak!" said Lily.

"Hello, Olivia!"

The little hamster ran to hug them.

When she saw the tearful kitten, she said,

"Anna, what's wrong?"

Lily explained about the Very Scary Cherries.

"Those wicked wolf cubs!" said Olivia. "We can't let them win — they're cheats!"

Lily nodded. "You're right. Can you think of a cherry that would reverse the Very Scary Cherry spell?"

Olivia put down her basket and looked along the rows of trees. "There's a Merry Cherry, a Cheery Cherry, a Worry Cherry ..." She shook her head. "No, that might make Anna worse. I'll look around."

As the girls examined labels on nearby

trees, Olivia scampered up and down the rows. Finally, she returned, shaking her head. "I don't think there's anything."

"What are we going to do?" Lily said in despair.

Anna sniffed. "There's nothing we can do. I'm too afraid. I wish I was plucky and brave."

Olivia stared at her. "Anna, that's it!" she cried. "Lucky Plucky Pears! They grow on a tree behind the blue-spotted cherry tree over there."

She darted away and returned with a knobbly green fruit. "Eat this, Anna."

The kitten buried her face beneath Jess's chin again. "I'm scared to try something new," she mewed.

"Lift me up, Lily, please," said Olivia. Lily put her hand flat on the ground for the hamster to climb on. Then she lifted her on to Jess's shoulder.

"Look, Anna," said Olivia. "It's perfectly OK. See?" She took a bite of the fruit. "Anna, we know you're afraid," said

Jess, "but we must win that Wishing Blossom if we're going to save Friendship Forest and get your teammates back."

Anna reached out a paw, took the Lucky Plucky Pear, and began to eat it. "Mmm ... tasty!" she said, taking another bite.

Almost at once, Anna's ears perked up. Her fur bristled and rippled. As she finished eating, Lily asked, "How do you feel? Are you brave enough for the Tumble Run?"

"Yes, I can do it!" said Anna.

"Then let's go," said Goldie. "It must be

nearly time for the race. Thank goodness the Lucky Plucky Pear worked!"

As they set off, Lily whispered to Jess, "Anna's definitely feeling braver now. I hope she feels as brave when she faces Team Snappyteeth!"

CHAPTER FOUR

The Jumping Tree

Anna ran ahead of Jess and Lily, and Goldie followed as fast as she could on her crutches. As they reached Sunshine Meadow, the Wishing Blossom began to glow.

There was a buzz of excitement as all the animals hurried to the starting line for

 97

the Tumble Run.

"Hurry!" said Lily. "Crash is heading for the start."

"Someone's already there," said Jess, "but it's not a wolf."

They ran to see who it was and were delighted to find a little fox cub.

"Ruby Fuzzybrush!" said Lily. "Are you racing, too?"

Ruby nodded. "I was too scared before, but I saw you beat Team Snappyteeth, so I know it can be done!"

Jess hugged the fox cub. "You're a good friend, Ruby!"

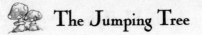

"Who's running for Flower Power?" asked Ruby.

"Me!" said Anna. "I'm feeling much braver now!"

She stood at the start line alongside Crash and Ruby. The watching animals cheered.

"Go, Ruby!"

"Two, four, six, eight, who's the cat

who's really great? ANNA!"

Smash, Dash and Flash jeered meanly but Anna ignored them.

"Rumble Tun obstacle race," Mr Cleverfeather announced, raising his flag. "Teddy, reams? I mean – ready, teams?" The racers nodded. He brought the flag down. "Go!"

Crash, Ruby and Anna sprang into action, all racing for the long, narrow

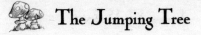

fence. Crash reached it first. He leaped on to it, closely followed by Anna, who had managed to overtake Ruby.

Anna kept looking down at the fence as she scurried along it.

"She's doing so well," Jess whispered.

"Keep going, Anna!" Lily yelled.

As the kitten gained on Crash, he glanced around.

"He looks worried," said Jess.

Goldie nodded. "He's probably scared of what Grizelda will do if he loses!"

Flash, Dash and Smash ran alongside the fence, shouting mean things at Anna.

"Wobbly legs!"

"Clumsy cat!"

"Slower than a snail!"

"They're horrible!" cried Jess. "Ignore them, Anna! They're just trying to scare you."

Anna lifted her tiny chin and leapt into the air. She sailed right over Crash

102

and landed on the fence ahead of him.

"She's in the lead!" Lily cheered as Anna leapt off the end of the fence and raced to the Jumping Tree. It had only three branches. There was one to the left at the bottom of the tree, one halfway up on the right and one at the very top, on the left. Lily and Jess could see that it would take three enormous jumps to get to the top of the tree!

As Anna paused at the bottom of the tree, Ruby Fuzzybrush overtook Crash.

"Hooray for Ruby!" yelled Jess, then everyone cheered Anna as she got ready.

Lily drew a breath. She'd seen how high Anna's first jump would have to be. She was nimble, but could she jump that far?

"Oh no!" cried Jess. "Look!"

While Crash was racing to catch up with Anna, Flash, Dash and Smash were climbing the Jumping Tree, using their claws to cling to the bark.

"Hey!" shouted Jess. "That's cheating!"

"What are those wicked wolf cubs up to?" groaned Goldie.

Lily frowned. "I don't know. But it can't be good!"

CHAPTER FIVE

Brave Little Anna

The three wolf cubs clung to the trunk of the Jumping Tree, where the racers had to jump from branch to branch to get across.

As Anna crouched, ready to jump to the first branch, Flash pulled it back, making the distance she needed to jump longer.

"Anna! Watch out!" Lily and Jess cried.

The kitten made her leap, landing safely on the branch.

"You did it!" cried Goldie.

The crowd cheered as Flash gave an annoyed growl. But there were more branches to come.

Anna crouched and sprang towards the next branch.

Lily gasped as Dash pulled that branch away. "She'll miss it!"

Anna gave a frightened mew as she clawed for a pawhold. "Meooooww!"

"She's falling!" cried Jess.

Anna just made the distance but didn't

manage to land

with all four paws.

She scrabbled at the

branch and was able

to hang on with her

front ones.

"She's OK!" said Lily.

There were more cheers as Anna

pulled herself up to safety, but cross

growls from Flash and Dash.

Ruby reached the bottom of the tree,

with Crash in hot pursuit. The little fox

cub made her first leap successfully. "Go

on, Anna!" she cried. "You can win! I

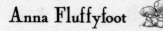

won't let Crash overtake me."

Anna paused. The third jump was the biggest of all.

"Watch out, Anna!" Jess shouted, as Smash pulled the next branch away.

Lily clutched Jess's hand. "Can she do it?"

Anna sprang, and seemed to almost fly through the air.

She landed safely, to more cheers.

As Anna made her way back down the tree, Ruby made her second jump and landed safely on the middle branch. Smash snarled at the fox cub and started

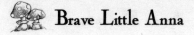

to shake the branch.

Ruby slipped and grabbed the trunk. "Aargh!" she cried.

"Careful!" Lily yelled.

But Ruby lost her grip and tumbled down to the next branch. She just managed to cling on by her front paws.

"Help!" she yelled. "I'm going to fall!"

"Oh no!" cried Goldie. "That's a long way for a little fox cub to tumble!"

Lily and Jess raced to the tree. But before they reached it, Anna shouted, "Hold on, Ruby!" and made a great leap towards the fox cub's branch.

Jess covered her eyes. "Did she make it?"

"She has!" cried Lily, as Anna landed and grasped Ruby's paw.

"I've got you!" Anna said.

With the kitten's help, Ruby scrambled back on to the branch.

"Thanks, Anna!" Ruby hugged her. "You saved me. But you'd better go if

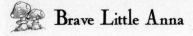

you're going to win the race! Quick!"

The girls and all the other animals cheered them both. "Hooray! Hooray!"

But the cheers changed to gasps as Crash jumped the last jump ... over Anna. He was winning!

"Oh no!" cried Jess. "Anna, run!"

The kitten leapt to the ground and raced for the next obstacle, the hollow tree trunk.

Crash was already through and, try as she might, Anna couldn't catch him up.

The wolf shot through the hollow tree trunk, out the other side, and straight

across the finish line.

As Team Snappyteeth leapt and
pranced and howled in excitement, the
girls rushed to comfort Anna, whose eyes
had filled with tears. "I lost the race."

"You did the right thing, helping
Ruby," said Lily.

"You're a true friend," Jess said.

Just then, Mr Cleverfeather announced, "The Tumble Run race has been won by Team Snappyteeth." He shook his feathers. "Dell wun." He seemed too sad to put his words right.

Lily held Anna's paw and Jess held Ruby's as they went back to the refreshment area with Goldie. Mrs Nibblesqueak had cool strawberry milkshakes waiting for them.

"I feel terrible," said Anna. "I've ruined everything."

"You saved your friend," said Goldie.

"That was a brave, unselfish thing to do. Anyway, the race score is one-all. There's another event to go, so we've still got a chance. Whoever wins the Tricky Tower race will win the Wishing Blossom."

"Let's hope it's Flower Power," said Ruby, hugging Anna.

"It will be!" said Lily. "Flower Power can still save Friendship Forest – and get Anna's teammates back!"

Story Three
Tricky Tower

CHAPTER ONE

Treasure Tree Trouble

Jess, Lily, Goldie and Anna crossed Sunshine Meadow to take a look at the Tricky Tower, where the next race would be held. It was round and very tall, and built of stone blocks. Lots of little coloured pebbles had been stuck to the stone blocks all over the tower.

With the score at one-all between Flower Power and Grizelda's Team Snappyteeth, this was the most important race of all. If the witch's team won, Grizelda would get the Wishing Blossom. And if she did, she would wish all the animals out of Friendship Forest.

Jess gazed up at the tower. "It's like a giant chimney," she said. "Do the climbers have to go all the way to the top?"

Goldie nodded. "It's not easy. They have to use the coloured pebbles as paw holds," she explained.

Anna's whiskers drooped. "Sophie

 118

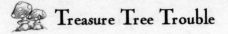

Flufftail the squirrel was going to be our climber," she said. "I haven't even practised this."

Jess stood next to the tower and put her hand on one of the pebbles. "Lily and I won't be able to stand in," she said with a frown. "Our hands are much too big to hold on to these."

The girls heard pounding hooves and spun around. A glossy brown Shetland pony was galloping towards them.

"Jess! Lily! Goldie!" she cried.

"It's Auntie Dappletrot!" said Jess. "She looks worried."

The pony slid to a stop. "I've just come from the Treasure Tree," she said, and paused to catch her breath.

The magical Treasure Tree was where the forest animals got much of their food. It grew every fruit and nut they needed.

"What's wrong?" asked Lily.

"You know the ropes that hang from

120

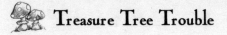

the tree to help the animals climb up?"
said Auntie Dappletrot. "Someone has cut
them."

There was only one person in
Friendship Forest mean enough to do
that. "Grizelda!" the girls said.

"That's not all," said Auntie Dappletrot.
"I heard cries for help coming from the
top of the tree. Some animals are stuck up
there."

Anna gasped. "It could be my
teammates – Hannah, Evie and Sophie!"

"There's only one way to find out," Jess
said. She glanced across at the Wishing

Blossom. It hadn't begun to glow yet, so
they still had time. "To the Treasure Tree!"
she cried. "And fast! We have to get back
before the Tricky Tower race."

Lily scooped Anna up, then remembered
that Goldie couldn't move that quickly
on her crutches. "Maybe you should wait
here," she suggested.

"Not while there are animals who
need my help," said Goldie. She turned to
the Shetland pony. "Auntie Dappletrot, I
wonder if you could help me?"

"Of course!" Auntie Dappletrot said
immediately. "Climb on my back and

hold on to my mane."

Jess helped Goldie up. "Ready, Auntie?" she said. "Then off we go!"

CHAPTER TWO

Rescue!

Several minutes later, Jess, Lily and Anna caught up with Auntie Dappletrot and Goldie at the huge Treasure Tree. As usual the branches were laden with every sort of fruit and nut imaginable. But beneath it lay untidy coils of rope.

Lily peered up into the tree and

saw flashes of black, white
and brown fur. "Evie?" she called.
"Hannah? Sophie? Is that you?"
There were faint cries. "Help us!"
came Sophie's voice. "We can't get
down and we're all tied up!"
Jess cupped her hands
around her mouth.
"Don't worry! We'll
rescue you!"
Lily sighed with

relief. "At least we know where your

teammates are, Anna."

"We'll have to climb up to them," said

Jess.

"It's a long way," Lily said. "It won't be

an easy climb."

"I wish my paw was better," Goldie said

dismally. "I'd climb that tree in two shakes

of a cat's tail."

Anna stuck out her little chin. "You

can't climb it, Goldie, but I can! I'm a cat,

too, so I'm a good climber. I'm going to
save my teammates!"

"We'll be right behind you," said Lily,
putting a coil of rope over her shoulder.
Jess did the same, and they wound more
ropes around their middles. "We'll use
these to bring your teammates down,"
Lily said.

Auntie Dappletrot gave a nervous
whinny. "Take care, all of you," she said.
"Goldie and I will watch out for Grizelda.
I'll stamp my hooves if she appears."

Anna, Jess and Lily began the long
climb. The girls found it easy to reach

the lower branches, so they helped Anna

through the tricky bits. As they got higher

and the branches grew thinner, Anna shot

ahead and was soon out of sight.

As the girls continued climbing, they

heard Anna cry out in dismay. Lily and

Jess exchanged

a worried

look and

scrambled

to the top

branches.

Evie, Hannah

and Sophie

were packed together into a large cage made from wood and sticks. The door was locked so they couldn't get out.

"We're so glad to see you," cried Evie.

"Grizelda's wicked spell whooshed us into this horrible cage," explained Sophie.

"Is it too late to stop her?" Hannah asked.

"No," said Anna as she struggled with a knot. "But we've got to hurry!"

Jess, Lily and Anna stood outside the cage. "After three," said Lily. "We'll pull the door from the outside and you push the door from the inside."

"One … two … three …"

The girls and Anna heaved while Evie, Hannah and Sophie pushed. With an almighty CRACK the wood snapped and the door swung open.

"We're free!" cried Sophie.

Anna hugged them each in turn and told them about the Petal Path and the Tumble Run.

"Wow," said Sophie. "You've done so well against those horrible wolves."

"It was mainly Anna," said Jess.

"No, it was all of us," said Anna. "We're a team."

The girls tied the ropes to strong branches. One after another, they all slid down to the ground.

"Whee!" cried Evie.

"Wa-hey!" shouted Hannah.

"Whoooop!" yelled Sophie.

Jess and Lily were last. They shot down, landing with a gentle bump beside Goldie and Auntie Dappletrot.

Goldie hugged Jess, Lily and Anna. "You've rescued the team! Now let's get back to Sunshine Meadow. We've got to make sure Team Flower Power win the Wishing Blossom!"

CHAPTER THREE

A Tricky Climb

The Flower Power team stood with Goldie and the girls, gazing up at the Tricky Tower. A green leaf-shaped flag fluttered from a platform at the top.

"That's high!" said Evie, with a gulp.

"You're very brave to be climbing it, Sophie," said Hannah Honeypaw.

"The race will start soon," Anna said to Sophie Flufftail. "Are you ready?"

The squirrel's tail was drooping and she looked fidgety. "I think you should do it, Anna."

The kitten was shocked. "Me?" she said. "But you're our best climber."

"My paws are stiff and sore from being tied together," said Sophie. "I don't think I can climb very well."

Anna's little mouth fell open, like she didn't know what to say.

"Anna, you can do it," said Hannah. "Look how fast you climbed the Treasure

Tree to rescue us."

Jess knelt beside the kitten. "Do you think you can do it, Anna?" she asked.

"Please," Lily added. "You're our best hope."

"I don't know …" Anna frowned in thought.

Just then, Team Snappyteeth sauntered over. "Little kitty thinks she can beat me, eh?" Smash sneered.

Anna glared and stuck out her chin again. "That does it," she said. "I'm climbing that tower!"

Lily hugged her. "We're so proud of you!"

Smash laughed. "Watch me, kitty. I'll be so far ahead, all you'll see is my tail!"

Jess said crossly, "Anna is a fantastic climber! She'll be in the lead in no time."

Crash snorted. "If she is, she'd better watch out. Smash might nip her paws!"

"That's cheating!" said Lily. Flash just stuck out her tongue.

From the other side of the field a cheer
rose up. The Wishing Blossom was lit!
It was time for the final race.

Mr Cleverfeather stepped
forward with his
flag. "The Tricky
Tower is – well,
tricky," he said,
"so nake tote
of sot I way. I
mean, take note
of what I say. Some
of the pebbles disappear when you touch
them. Some pebbles will boost you up.

 137

Others will make you slip down."

"Mr Cleverfeather," Lily said, "how can the climbers tell which pebble boosts and which pebble slips?"

The owl shook his head. "Nobody can tell. It's part of the magic."

Jess thought the Tricky Tower sounded rather like Snakes and Ladders, her dad's favourite board game. But in this version you didn't know which pebble was a snake and which was a ladder. This sounded very tricky.

Mr Cleverfeather raised his flag. "Teddy, reams? I mean, ready, teams?"

Jess and Lily held their breath. The fate
of the forest depended on Anna winning.

Mr Cleverfeather's flag swished down.
"Go!"

Smash and Anna jumped off the
ground and began to climb. Anna's tiny
paws easily gripped the pebbles. She got
off to a great start.

But Smash was bigger and stronger.
She could reach further with her long legs
and haul herself up easily. Soon they were
neck and neck.

"Go, Anna!" cried the crowd.

Lily clutched Jess's hand. "I wish we

could help."

"Flower Power's a team," said Goldie. "You can help."

"How?" asked Jess.

There were cheers as Anna scrambled ahead of Smash. Her tail swished as she

chose a pebble that boosted her up. Now she was much higher than the cub.

"Look at the pebbles," said Goldie. "Work out which ones help them up, and which ones make them slip down. Then you can tell Anna which to go for."

Jess and Lily concentrated hard. Every time a pebble made the climbers slip or boosted them up, they remembered what it looked like.

"Goldie," said Jess, "see the pebbles with a knobbly bit in the middle?"

Goldie squinted hard at the tower. "Yes," she said.

"I think they're the ones that boost you up!" Jess finished.

"And the ones with rounded corners make you slip down!" Lily said excitedly. "Now we can help Anna!"

The climbers were more than halfway up, with Anna just in the lead. The kitten was already reaching for the next pebble – a smooth one …

"Not that one, Anna!" the girls yelled together.

But it was too late. Anna's paw reached the pebble – and immediately, she slipped. She cried out and slid down the tower.

 142

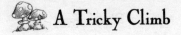

"No!" cried Evie, Hannah and Sophie
in horror.

Then, just before she hit the ground,
Anna's paws grabbed on to a pebble. Lily
and Jess drew sighs of relief.

"You'll have to start again, you silly
little kitty!" jeered Dash. He gave a howl

of delighted laughter.

"You're winning now!" Crash shouted up to Smash. "This will be easy!"

The crowd fell silent. Everyone knew what would happen if Smash reached the top first. Grizelda would get the Wishing Blossom, and Friendship Forest would be doomed.

CHAPTER FOUR

Grizelda Returns

Anna was clinging tightly to the pebble she'd grabbed. Above her, Smash climbed higher and higher.

"I'll never catch up!" the kitten cried.

"You will," said Lily. "Just do as we say!"

"We'll work as a team," said Jess.

"Just like we did with the Petal Path, remember?"

Anna nodded determinedly. She reached for the green pebble directly above her. It had rounded corners.

"Not that one!" said Lily. "Go up and left – yes, grab that knobbly one!"

Anna grasped it with her paw. She shot up in the air towards the next group of pebbles.

"The knobbly ones boost you!" Jess called. "The next one's on your left!"

The kitten's ears twitched as the girls called out directions. They told her where

 146

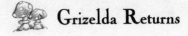

the knobbly pebbles were, and stopped her from grabbing the smooth ones that would make her slip. Anna made her way up the tower, her paws fumbling for the knobbly pebbles. Her tail swished, helping her to balance. As she got boosted up again and again, her confidence seemed to grow and she climbed faster.

"You're gaining on Smash!" Goldie cried.

"Go, Anna!" the crowd shouted. "An-na! An-na!"

Smash grabbed a smooth pebble and slipped down with a shocked yelp. She scrabbled for a pawhold but, by the time she managed to get a grip, Anna had overtaken her. The kitten leapt up from pebble to pebble, climbing easily.

Everyone cheered!

"Go, Anna!" her teammates yelled.

Jess and Lily hugged each other excitedly. "She's winning!"

 148

Goldie gasped and pointed across the
meadow with her wooden crutch. "Look!"

A yellow-green orb of light was
speeding towards them.

"Grizelda!" cried Lily. "Oh no!"

The animals huddled nervously
together. Jess and Lily stood in front of
Evie, Hannah and Sophie. They didn't
want anything else happening to the poor

creatures now that they had been rescued.

"What's happening?" Anna called down.

"Grizelda's here!" Goldie shouted.

"You keep climbing, Anna," Jess called. "We'll take care of her!"

The orb burst in a shower of stinking sparks, and there stood the witch.

"Go away, Grizelda," Lily said.

"No!" Grizelda snapped. "I've come to make sure little kitty loses. Ha haa!"

"No you won't!" Jess shouted angrily. "Anna is going to win, fair and square!"

"That's right," said Lily, wishing she

was as sure as she sounded. "Team Flower Power will win the Wishing Blossom."

Grizelda cackled. "Haa! We'll see about that. Crash! Flash! Dash!"

The wolf cubs slunk over to the witch.

"Where should I go next?" Anna called down.

Jess carried on guiding Anna to the right pebbles while Lily and Goldie kept an eye on Grizelda

151

and Team Snappyteeth. The cubs were quiet, but Lily saw Grizelda's lips moving.

"She's casting a spell!" Lily whispered. "But I can't hear what she's chanting."

"Not that one, Anna!" Jess was calling up to the kitten, who had reached for a smooth pebble. "Get that knobbly one above you. It'll boost you right to the top!"

Anna reached for the knobbly pebble. But the moment she touched it, she tumbled down, down, down!

Jess gave a cry of horror. Lily and Goldie whirled around to see Anna

falling. The crowd gasped in dismay.

Grizelda and Team Snappyteeth screeched with laughter. "Who's winning now?" Grizelda cackled.

Anna scrabbled for a pawhold, and managed to grab hold of a pebble halfway down the tower.

The crowd whooped.

"Carry on winning, Smash!" Grizelda yelled. "I'll sit under the Wishing Tree until it's time to pick that blossom. Ha! Friendship Forest will soon be mine!"

Jess was dismayed. "What happened? I'm sure that pebble was knobbly."

Lily grabbed Jess's arm. "I know what must have happened," she said. "Grizelda has reversed the pebbles' powers!"

"You're right!" cried Goldie.

"Anna!" Jess shouted. "Grab that smooth pebble!"

Anna peered down at them, her eyes wide with worry. "The smooth one? Won't I slip?"

"Grizelda's changed the pebbles!" Jess called. "Go up again! Now left!"

Every time she grabbed a smooth pebble, Anna was boosted further up the tower. Soon, she was gaining on Smash.

On the ground, Dash,
Crash and Flash had their
ears pricked with worry.

"Up and left!" Dash
yelled to Smash.

"Straight up!" Crash
shouted at the same time.

"Go right!" yelled
Flash.

"Make up your minds!"
Smash shouted down to
them.

Anna had just one
more pebble to go

before she'd be at the top of the tower.
"You need that smooth one on your left!"
Jess called.

The girls held their breath.

Anna reached for the pebble. The
moment she touched it – whoosh!

She was boosted up so far that she
landed on all fours on the platform at the
top of the tower.

"Hooray!" everyone cheered.

Anna grabbed the flag fluttering there
and punched the air. "Flower Power!" she
cried. "We've done it!"

CHAPTER FIVE

Just One Wish

Jess, Lily, Hannah, Evie and Sophie
danced around with a very happy Goldie.

Anna had not only won the Friendship
Forest Sports Day prize for her team,
she'd saved the forest from Grizelda! All
the animals cheered as she waved the flag
from the top of Tricky Tower.

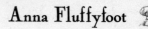

"Anna!" Mr Cleverfeather called. "The stones are normal now! You can dime clown safely – I mean climb down safely."

When Anna reached the ground, Team Flower Power hugged her.

"Well done!" they cried.

A horrible screech of "Nooooo!" made them all cover their ears.

Grizelda charged across the meadow, sending the animals scurrying away in fear. "You must have cheated, nasty kitty!" Her face was purple with rage.

"You're the cheater," cried Jess. "And cheaters never win!"

...

"Pah!" Grizelda shook her fists. "You wait! Friendship Forest will be mine one day. You'll see! Especially you horrible girls!" She glared at Team Snappyteeth and snarled, "I'm finished with wolves!" She snapped her fingers, disappearing

in a burst of sparks.

Everyone in Sunshine Meadow cheered and gathered around.

"Hooray!"

"You beat Grizelda!"

Lily grinned. "If we work as a team, we will always be able to stop Grizelda."

That brought the loudest cheer of all!

In Sunshine Meadow, happy animals celebrated Sports Day and the defeat of Grizelda. Friendship Forest was safe!

The refreshment stalls formed one long picnic feast. Animals started at one end with cherry tomato and cheese tartlets, then went on to toasted sesame seed and honey biscuits. They kept going until they reached the Prettywhiskers' stall, with ten flavours of their Purrfect Ice Cream.

The wolf cubs sulked beneath a tree.

Jess, Lily, Goldie and Anna enjoyed blueberry and lemon cupcakes and chatted about Anna's wish.

"Now my teammates are back, I don't know what to wish for," said Anna.

Mr and Mrs Snuffynose came over.

"We still haven't found our pups," Mrs Snuffynose said anxiously. "They've been gone for hours."

"Oh no," said Lily. "Perhaps Grizelda hid them somewhere else?"

The dogs' eyes widened with worry.

"We'll search for them," said Jess.

"There are lots of puppies around, though. What do yours look like?"

"Dusty has a patch over his eye," said Mr Snuffynose. "Floss has a white ear …"

His wife continued, "Crackle has a stumpy tail and Sasha has different-coloured eyes."

Lily glanced at Jess. "Hey, doesn't Dash have a patch over his eye?"

"Yes," said Jess. "And doesn't Flash have a stumpy tail?"

"And Crash has different-coloured eyes," Goldie added.

Suddenly they all realised the truth.

"The Snuffynose puppies are the wolf cubs!" cried Lily, pointing to where Team Snappyteeth sat under the tree. "Even their names are similar!"

"Grizelda must have put a spell on them," said Goldie.

Just then Mr Cleverfeather hooted. "Teddle mime! I mean, medal time!"

Jess and Lily told the Snuffynoses they would try to change the puppies back after the ceremony. They joined the animals at the winners' podium, under the Wishing Tree.

Mr Cleverfeather announced, "The

champions are … Team Flower Power!"

"Hooray!" everyone cheered, as the
teammates pushed Anna on to the
podium.

"Anna must have the wish!" said Evie.

"Look up, Anna dear," said Mrs
Cleverfeather, who had come to help.

Above the kitten's head, the Wishing

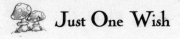

Blossom lit up.

"What will you wish for?" quacked Ellie Featherbill the duckling.

Anna smiled. "I know exactly what I'll wish for." She reached up, plucked the shining flower and closed her eyes. "I wish for Team Snappyteeth to turn back into the Snuffynose puppies!"

Beneath the lime tree, there was a flurry of golden, crackling sparks.

In the wolf cubs' place sat four rather surprised puppies. They ran to their mum and dad.

"We're us again!" cried Sasha, and

the whole family became a tangle of hugging paws and wagging tails.

"Thanks to Anna's wish!" said Jess.

The puppies nearly bowled the kitten over in their rush to hug and thank her.

When they'd calmed down, Dusty said, "Sorry we were so mean."

Lily stroked him. "It wasn't your fault. It's Grizelda who's mean."

Mr Cleverfeather hooted again. "Will Evie, Sophie, Hannah, Goldie, Less and Jilly join Anna on the podium?"

Mrs Cleverfeather presented each Flower Power teammate with a medal

 166

and a peck on the cheek.

The winners waved to the

crowd. Jess and Lily were thrilled with

their medals. On the front they said

'Winner'. On the back was 'Friendship',

surrounded by pawprints.

Soon it was time for the girls

to say goodbye. They hugged

Anna, and promised to come

back soon.

Goldie rode on Auntie

Dappletrot to the Friendship Tree. Then

Lily helped her down so she could touch

the tree to make the door appear.

"We hope your paw will be better soon," said Jess, hugging her.

"I'm sure it will," said Goldie. "Goodbye, girls. Thank you for saving our forest once again."

"You can count on us," said Lily.

The girls waved to Auntie Dappletrot, opened the door and stepped into the golden glow. The tingle told them they were returning to their proper size.

When the light faded, Jess and Lily were back in Brightley Meadow. They ran back to Helping Paw together.

"Let's help Mum and Dad finish the

stable," said Lily. "It'll be much quicker if we work together."

Jess grinned. "Team Helping Paw!"

There wasn't much left to do. Lily was just hanging up a golden horseshoe when Mr Hart called, "Starshine's arrived!"

Minutes later, Tom the trainer unloaded a glossy brown horse from her horsebox.

Lily stroked her long chestnut neck. "Hello, Starshine. You're beautiful."

Tom nodded. "And she's been a great racer. She's won lots of prizes. Cups, shields, medals … We made a good team, didn't we, girl?"

Jess smiled at Lily. They had, too!

Tom leaned his face against the horse's cheek. "It wasn't just the winning," he said. "We've been together for years. I'll miss you, Starshine, but you'll be happy at Helping Paw."

The girls smiled at each other. They knew, too, that friendship was worth more than prizes.

And they couldn't wait to see all their forest friends again!

The End

Jess and Lily are heading to the enchanted
Spelltop School! Can they stop Grizelda
from spoiling the magic?

Turn over for a sneak peek of the next
adventure,

Charlotte Waggytail
Learns a Lesson

"These pups are so adorable!" exclaimed Jess Forester. She and her best friend, Lily Hart, were in Lily's back garden. The autumn sunshine was warm on their backs. They were sitting in a wooden pen, playing with three tiny, golden puppies with flappy ears and curly tails.

"Someone handed them in to Helping Paw this morning," said Lily.

Lily's parents were vets, and they ran the Helping Paw Wildlife Hospital from a converted barn at the bottom of their garden. Lily and Jess spent every minute they could caring for the animal patients.

Jess scooped up the smallest puppy and giggled as it nibbled her blonde hair. It felt warm and soft in her arms. "They're unusual," she said. "What breed are they?"

"I'm not sure." Lily opened a book that lay at her feet. "I asked Mum and Dad, but they don't know either, so I got this book about dog breeds from the library."

Jess put her pup gently on the grass and bent over the book. "These puppies have squashy black noses like pugs but their ears are floppier." The pup pulled at her trainer laces. "Hey, don't do that, you cheeky thing!" Lily said with a giggle.

She rolled the bone across the pen. To her surprise, a paw poked out from under a blanket and batted the toy back.

A cat with gleaming golden fur crawled out from the blanket. She stretched and gave a friendly miaow.

"Goldie!" cried Lily.

Read

Charlotte Waggytail
Learns a Lesson

to find out what happens next!

Magic
Animal Friends

Look out for the brand-new
Magic Animal Friends series!

Series Seven

www.magicanimalfriends.com

Magic
Animal Friends
Can you keep the secret?

There's lots of fun for everyone at
www.magicanimalfriends.com

Play games and explore the secret world of
Friendship Forest, where animals can talk!

Join the
Magic Animal Friends Club!

–✕ Special competitions –✕
–✕ Exclusive content –✕
–✕ All the latest Magic Animal Friends news! –✕

To join the Club, simply go to

www.magicanimalfriends.com/join-our-club/

Terms and Conditions
(1) Open to UK and Republic of Ireland residents only (2) Please get the email of your parent/guardian to enter
(3) We may use your data to contact you with further offers

Full terms and conditions at www.hachettechildrensdigital.co.uk/terms/